# Jack
## and the
# Beanstalk

and me!

For Charles, Samuel and Emilia – E.B.

First published 2015 by Nosy Crow Ltd
The Crow's Nest, 10a Lant Street
London SE1 1QR
www.nosycrow.com
ISBN 978 0 85763 472 6 (HB)
ISBN 978 0 85763 473 3 (PB)
Nosy Crow and associated logos are trademarks
and/or registered trademarks of Nosy Crow Ltd
Text © Nosy Crow 2015
Illustrations © Nosy Crow 2014
The right of Ed Bryan to be identified as the
illustrator of this work has been asserted.

A CIP catalogue record for this book is available from the British Library.
Printed in China
Papers used by Nosy Crow are made from wood grown in
sustainable forests.
1 3 5 7 9 8 6 4 2 (HB)
3 5 7 9 8 6 4 2 (PB)

# Jack
## and the
# Beanstalk

 nosy crow

Illustrated by
Ed Bryan

Once upon a time, there was a boy called **Jack** who lived with his mother in a tiny little cottage. They were **very** poor.

Jack was a **good** boy, and he was very **brave**, but he didn't always think things through.

One day, Jack's mother asked her son to take their **COW** to the market. "We have nothing to eat and no money," she said. "We **have** to sell Daisy."

Jack **fed** Daisy, **cleaned** her
and put a **bell** around her neck,
then he set off for the market.

Jack and Daisy had not gone very far before they met a strange-looking man with an old **suitcase**.

"Hello, young man," said the stranger. "What a **lovely cow** you've got! If you give her to me, you can have ten of these **magic beans.**"

Magic Beans

"How **exciting!**" Jack replied. "I'll take them!"

But when Jack got home and showed his mother the beans, she was **very** angry.

"I can't believe you swapped our **only cow** for these ridiculous **beans!**" she shouted.

"But they're **magic beans!**" Jack cried.
"They're not magic, you **silly** boy!" said his mum,
and she threw the beans out of the window.

The very next morning, when Jack woke up, he found an **enormous** beanstalk in his garden. He decided to climb to the very top!

Jack climbed **higher**
and **higher**
and **higher.**

The beanstalk seemed
to go on **forever!**

At last, Jack reached the **top** of the beanstalk. To his amazement, a long path led to a **huge castle** in the clouds!

Jack walked up to the castle doors and went inside.

Straight away, a little
mouse ran up to Jack.
"This is the giant's castle,"
it said. "He's scary!"

"I'm not afraid of giants!"
said Jack. "I'm going to
have a look around."

The first room Jack found was the **kitchen**, where a **cook** was making soup. **"Please,** can you help me?" said the cook. "The giant wants his **lunch!"**

Jack chopped the vegetables and stirred the ingredients. Soon the soup smelled **delicious**.

"**Oh, thank you,**" said the cook. "Because you've helped me, I'll tell you where the giant keeps his stolen **gold**."

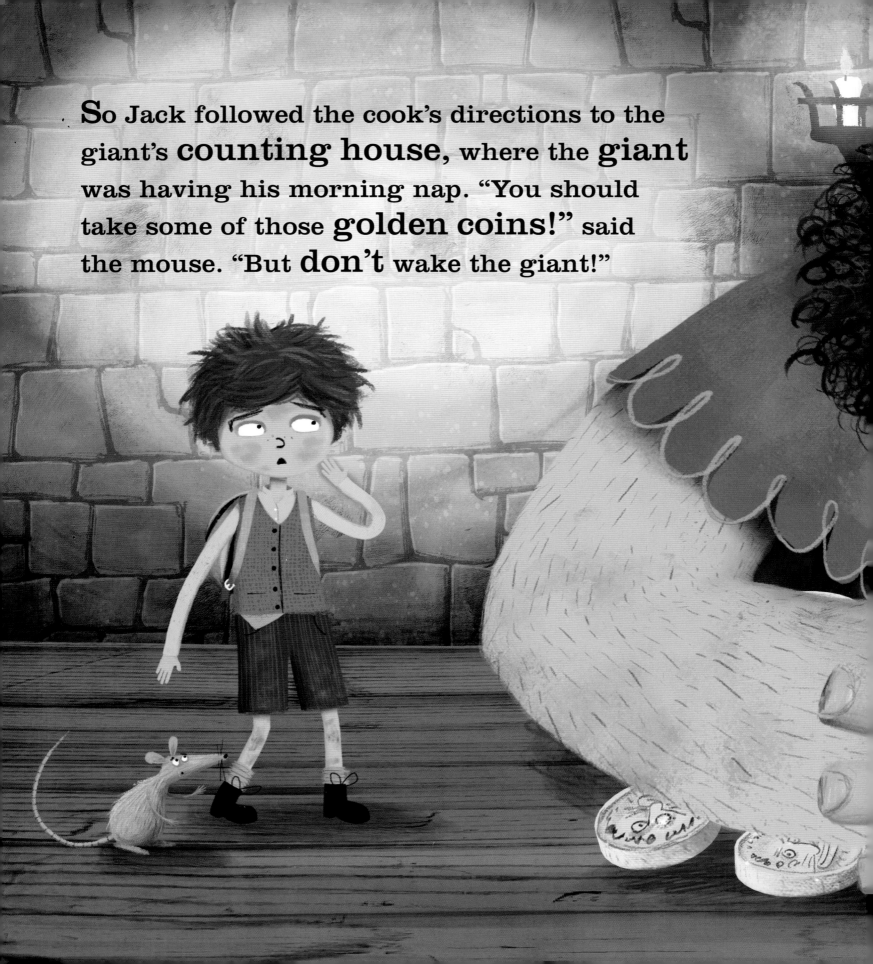

So Jack followed the cook's directions to the giant's **counting house**, where the **giant** was having his morning nap. "You should take some of those **golden coins!**" said the mouse. "But **don't** wake the giant!"

ZZZZ z z z

Jack **carefully** lifted
the giant's hands and took
the **coins.** He stuffed
them into his bag then
crept out of the room.

Jack kept exploring. Soon he found a room where a **frog** sat by a **well**.

"**Please**, can you help me?" said the frog. "The giant stole my **golden ball** and threw it down this well!"

Jack lowered the **bucket** into the well, scooped up
the ball and wound the bucket up again.
The frog **hopped** for joy.

"**Oh, thank you**," said the frog.
"Because you've helped me, I'll tell you where
the giant keeps his stolen **magic goose**."

So Jack went to the **goosery**, where the **giant** was sleeping after his lunch.

"One of these geese lays **golden eggs**," said the mouse, "but which one? Whatever you do, **don't** wake the giant!"

Jack lifted each goose,
one after the other, until
he found a **golden egg!**
He tucked the egg and the
goose into his bag, then
crept out of the room.

Underneath the castle, Jack found the **dungeon**,
where a **baby dragon** was locked up in a cell.
**"Please,** can you help me?" said the dragon.
"I'm just a baby and I want to go **home** to my mum!"

Jack took the **big iron key** off its hook on the wall, turned it in the lock and **freed** the baby dragon.

**"Oh, thank you,"** said the dragon. "Because you've helped me, I'll tell you where the giant keeps his stolen **golden harp.**"

So Jack made his way to the **music room** where the giant was having **another** nap! **"Please,** can you help me?" said a little golden harp. "I want to escape from the giant. He's so **mean."**

Jack picked up the harp, but it suddenly started to shout.

"I tricked you!" it screeched.

"I'm going to call my master now!

Master Giant,
wakey **wakey!**

This boy Jack is trying

to **take** me!"

The giant woke up and glared around him.
"Fee, fi, fo, fum," he boomed.
"I can smell you! Here I come!"

The giant **chased** Jack
through the castle.

"You may think that you're
the **winner,** but I'll eat you up
for **dinner!**" shouted the giant.

The giant **chased** Jack down the beanstalk.

"You can try to **run away,** but I'll eat you up **today!**" the giant yelled.

When Jack reached the ground, he grabbed
an **axe** and chopped the beanstalk down.
It toppled over with a loud **CRASH!**

The giant was **never** seen or heard of again. And as for Jack and his mother, they both lived **happily** ever after.